The Chameleon

THE CHAMELEON

A Comedy in Three Acts

BY

JOSEPHINE PRESTON PEABODY
(MRS. LIONEL MARKS)

NEW YORK
SAMUEL FRENCH
PUBLISHER
28-30 WEST 38TH STREET

LONDON
SAMUEL FRENCH, LTD.
26 SOUTHAMPTON STREET
STRAND

THE CHAMELEON.

CHARACTERS.

JUSTIN AURELIUS HOPEFAR *Philosopher; young, unwed*

RUFUS HOPEFAR } *Unphilosophic; but wed*
} *His brothers.*
WALTER HOPEFAR } *Unphilosophic; Unwed*

REV. INGRAHAM SYLVESTER..*Reverend, but not so very*

QUENTIN CARRICK.............*A Man of Letters*

JAMES ROBERTS THOMAS, Ph. D.
MAJOR KILMAYNE
THOMAS.................*The Hopefars' butler*
HONORA THORPE......*A New Woman and Young*
ROSE HOPEFAR................*Young; not New*
MRS. RANDAL VAN WYCK...........*Never New*
MRS. HOPEFAR-SHUTTLEWORTH........*Never Old*

THE CHAMELEON

PLACE:—*Out of town.*

TIME:—*The present.*

Three months elapse between ACTS I *and* II. ACTS II *and* III *are concerned with the events of thirty-six hours.*

ACT   I. *Morning.   How truth is green and lovely.*

ACT II. *Afternoon.   How truth is gray and dismal.*

ACT III. SCENE I. *Night.   How truth is rainbow, truth is piebald.*

SCENE II. *Morning.   How you may catch a Chameleon, if you get up early.*

SCENE *throughout:—The* HOPEFAR *Library.*

THE CHAMELEON

———

ACT I.

SCENE:—*The* HOPEFARS' *Library. A large, old-fashioned place, evidently built out in a separate wing, from the house, into which it opens, left at back, with a few steps, and a doorway. The only other entrance is the centre-door, at back, (of glass, with straight hangings) which gives upon the garden.* R. *and* L. *of this door, French windows opening on a terrace walk with a high hedge. Book-lined walls.*

RIGHT, *an open fireplace; and* R. *and* L. *of the fireplace, two Chinese cabinets, with drawers and pigeon-holes. Near by, but up stage at present, a long, high-backed sofa, the end near the windows concealed by a screen folded across,* R. C. *Down, some half-unpacked book-boxes, covered with foreign labels.*

LEFT, *below the house-steps, a large bust of Hermes on a pedestal. Towards the front, a writing-table strewn with work.*
As the curtain rises, the garden-door stands open, and one window, R. *It is a bright June morning.*

(*Enter* L. *from the house,* ROSE HOPEFAR; *and the* REVEREND SYLVESTER *with his hat and stick.*

He beams with all the satisfaction of forty-
five and well-to-do. ROSE *is young and discon-*
tented.)

REVEREND. —Not at all,—not at all! Really a
pleasure, I assure you. If only you had told me all
about it much earlier you know, I could, perhaps—
ah—have set the matter before her in its—ah—true
light. She has such a singularly fresh and candid—
ah—nature; it is sure to—ah—respond to the candid *word in time.*

ROSE. (*With a sigh of darkest prophecy*) Ah!

REVEREND. And it is with words as with stitches,
dear Lady. (L.) A word in time—saves Nine!

ROSE. (*Earnestly*) But what would be the
use—Oh! Nine swear-words, you mean.

REVEREND. (*Hastily*) Not at all,—not at——

ROSE. Do tell her that. I felt sure your sense of
humor would appeal to her. She used to have so
much. (*Looking towards the terrace*) She ought
to be here by this. It's growing late.—Ah, you will
persuade her! It's a terrible thing to all of us, that
she should have thrown him over. (*Looking out*)

REVEREND. (*Crosses* R.) Of course, of course.
Poor Walter.

ROSE. (*Comes down*) And aside from all
graver considerations, you know, a June wedding
would have been so lovely! I must say, (*Sits* L) it
was a curious time to jilt him.—I had talked about
her as my sister-in-law for months. And the brides-
maids' gowns were entirely planned.

REVEREND. Not really!

ROSE. Their hats, too. I designed them. And
Justin came back from Egypt for the wedding.

REVEREND. Justin home? And with a new book
ready?

ROSE. Oh, that book!—Yes, almost ready. He
came early, to be here well before. And while he

was sailing home, for his own brother's wedding, Honora changed her mind. Think of it:—their Hats!—

REVEREND. It sounds alarmingly unfeminine. What does Justin think of her?

ROSE. He hasn't seen her. He came only yesterday, you see; and he's deep in that Book. It's all very nice—rather piquant, indeed, to have a well-known man of letters for a brother-in-law. People want to meet him and all that. But you can't expect him to be useful in other ways. What do you think his new book is called?—"*Aspects of Truth.*"

REVEREND. Him.—"Aspects"—Essentially modern.

ROSE. As if we should ever know what Truth was, if we stopped to consider its "aspects". Surely (*Earnestly*) it's the aspects of things that obscure the truth. I mean to say, you can only be sure of the Truth, when you speak on impulse. For if you stop to think it out at all, you're so apt to say something else. Do you see what I mean?

REVEREND. Quite so,—quite so. (*He inspects* R. *some of the unpacked books, title by title, with disapproval*)

ROSE. Oh, these writers of books, what do they know about Life? And the serious side of the matter is:—do you know what explains the whole thing?

REVEREND. (*Turns and sits on step-ladder*) Dear lady, which? Life or Honora?

ROSE. Honora, jilting my own brother-in-law!

REVEREND. Give me a clue.

ROSE. *Honora* is writing a book.

REVEREND. Honora!

ROSE. I knew you'd think just that. And so do I. Of course I always knew she was fearfully clever. But I was too fond of her ever to believe it would take that shape. I thought she would marry.

REVEREND. A book, dear me! What does she call it?

ROSE. "*The Chameleon,*" she says.

REVEREND. "*The Chameleon!*"

ROSE. And of course you know Honora well enough to know it can have nothing in the world to do with chameleons.

REVEREND. Quite so.

ROSE. She doesn't like them, you know. She never would wear the one I gave her that season, when we all wore them, hopping on a little gold chain. But the serious side of the matter is that she never would have thrown Walter over, if it had not been for that book. She was *turning literary;* and we never saw it! And here she has been, reading, reading, writing, writing, hours at a time; and making up her mind that she didn't care to marry Walter after all. Of course, we're close neighbors; and she always did like this old place. Nobody uses it when Justin is away. And I'm devoted to Honora. But—(*Sees a card on the table, and picks it up, interrupting herself*) "Mr. Carrick." What a pity: and I was close by, out in the summerhouse. As I was saying; even for such an old friend, it was cold-blooded of her, to sit here writing herself out of that state of mind; practically to jilt Walter in his own library! Why doesn't she come? (*She stirs about, righting small objects on the table*) I did want to see her settled, and happy. I even wanted her, really wanted her in our family. And now she is going to be literary! (*She goes towards the screen to fold it back*) How warm it is! And everything upsidedown.

REVEREND. Allow me.

(*They fold it back together, disclosing the settle, which stands with its back towards the audience, slanted* R. *up* C. *At the upper end of it is visible the top of a large white garden-hat with*

*long strings of mull, and an edge of scarf. The
hat wears an air of lazy abandon. Both recoil,
dismayed.)*

ROSE. Really, Honora! I have said nothing that
I—that I can possibly recall. But I think you might
have spoken before this! (*She turns superbly, and
sweeps across, up the steps and into the house, clos-
ing the door.* SYLVESTER *crosses after her; then
recovers his composure*)

REVEREND. (*At the house steps*) Ah, dear Mrs.
Hopefar, won't you stay? I beg of you. As you
will, then. (*Urbanely*) Honora and I are to have
a quiet little talk, and to set things once for all in
their true light. The truth, the truth, at any cost!
(*He regards the hat expectantly, standing down* C.)
Come.—I was sure, my dear Child, that you felt this
all more keenly than anyone seems to believe. Don't
suffer in silence. Mind you, I don't wish to intrude.
But tell me all your doubts; and let us resolve them
completely. It is never too late. And with words—
(*Advances winningly*) It is sometimes with words
as with stitches, Honora. A word in time saves
Nine! Ha, ha. My dear girl, you are not weeping?
(*Crosses* R., *starts; then with an expression of
disgust, removes the hat from the parasol-handle
which had held it in place. There is no one sit-
ting there. He looks on considers*) Hm! *There
is a sound of whistling without. Schubert's Unfin-
ished Symphony theme.* REV. *slowly and prophet-
ically*) Whistling girls and hens that crow!
(*Enter* C., *from the garden,* JUSTIN HOPEFAR. *He

   is a young man of abundant cheerfulness and
   some distinction. He wears a straw-hat and
   carries a pipe.*)

JUSTIN. Sylvester! How are you. I would
have known that back in Patagonia.

REVEREND. Justin, my dear fellow! I mistook you for Honora.

JUSTIN. Have I changed so much? We may look alike for aught I know. (*Lays hat on table*) I hear that I must have seen Honora once, when she was small and harmless. But I don't remember. And it doesn't matter, for it seems that now at the eleventh hour, she rejects us all. (*Relights his pipe*) It has set the household by the ears though. Are you come to hold parley with Honora?

REVEREND. Yes. She was to see me here a little while this morning, to see if I could not settle her untimely doubts. Her own family, you know is much distressed. She has no fault to find with Wat; she cares for no one else. It must be readjusted. But where's Honora?

JUSTIN. And what's that flag of truce?

REVEREND. Oh, that's her Hat. (*He hangs it on the white parasol and they both inspect it dreamily*)

JUSTIN. Her Hat, " untenanted of its mistress?" I say. It fills me with suspense, somehow.—Is Honora becoming to her Hat?

REVEREND. Eminently. But I fear she is a New Woman. (*Turns away*)

JUSTIN. (*Taking the parasol and lifting it, cautiously*) Never mind. If she keeps on wearing such hats. In any case, I suspect the New Woman isn't new. She is only more numerous at present. She's a thoroughly logical outcome. I won't quarrel with her till I understand her. . . . Now, why those long streamers?

REVEREND. Can't imagine.

JUSTIN. It's something new, some hitching device instead of apron-strings, you may be sure. A Hat without a woman; like a man without a Country. A Hat,—like the sleeping lion, shorn of all its terrors.

(Sudden singing outside. HONORA passes the window up R. JUSTIN guiltily transfers the parasol and hat to the hands of SYLVESTER who clutches them absent-mindedly. They stand still as HONORA enters hatless, C. with an armful of green balsam boughs. She comes swinging in, exuberantly and checks herself as she sees them.)

HONORA. Oh! *(She hastily goes to the fireplace and deposits there the load of greenery; then turns back, dusting off her hands softly. JUSTIN looks at her fixedly)*

REVEREND. Good-morning, Honora! *(Jauntily)* Here is Justin, . . . your brother-in-law elect.

(She shakes hands with JUSTIN; but looking him in the eyes, with a smiling negative head-shake.)

JUSTIN. You don't remember me? But please stay. Of course I'm going away at once.

HONORA. No. Don't go away, Justin. It's a strange kind of introduction. But you'd much better stay. Look at the truth of it from the beginning, and see what kind of a sister you are not to have. And you'll bless me for not marrying him. Yes, indeed, it's I,—this is how I've grown up. *(As he looks at her intently)*

JUSTIN. I see. And do you keep on growing?

HONORA. *(Exuberantly)* Forever!

REVEREND. Hm!

JUSTIN. I wonder what you'll be like, seven years from now.

HONORA. Come and see; if we're still neighbors.

REVEREND. Hm! My dear, Justin, this is all very interesting to consider. But I had an engagement to lunch, and whether they're still neighbors I hardly——

HONORA. But surely, Reverend dear, you don't need to wear my hat?

(REVEREND *still clutching the hat in one hand and the parasol in the other, crosses to center.*)

REVEREND. I—I—dear me, Honora! I was try-ing to fathom the mazes of your mind by— You may remember that I came this morning to talk with you about certain distressing——

JUSTIN. *Au revoir!* (*Taking his own hat*)

HONORA. Don't go. Well then, just outside. It's only right that you should hear, if you all think I'm so unreasonable; and that I don't know my own mind. I believe you'd be fair.—And I may need you yet.

JUSTIN. You have only to speak. (*Exit* c. *He is seen on the terrace, just outside the window sit-ting with his pipe*)

HONORA. (*Hospitably*) Now then! Tell me all about how horrid I am!

REVEREND. (*Sits down* L. C.) Honora, you well know that you are singularly far from horrid.—But you *are* unreasonable, untimely and exasperat-ing.

HONORA. I? — Reverend? — Justin! (JUSTIN *turns*) No, no, Justin; it was a weak appeal. Rev-erend, I never heard you phrase anything so di-rectly. Now, if you would only do that in your sermons, you know, Reverend dear, I'd come to hear them—positively on week-days. I would.

REVEREND. (*Resignedly*) Ah! Get around me, now. Begin!

HONORA. Upon my word, why will nobody re-spect *my* search for Truth? (JUSTIN *wheels his chair about and looks in*) Why will nobody under-stand that I've grown up suddenly,—tardily, if you like; and that I must needs seem mulish about all

manner of things; what I love, and what I
hate?

REVEREND. Love? What do you love, Honora?

HONORA. I only wish I knew.

REVEREND. What do you hate?

HONORA. *Pretenses! Big or little.* Compro-
mise. Old make-believes. Life, at hear-say. Half-
way things, gray things, not black, not white.
Everything, everything, everything except——

REVEREND. What, Honora?

HONORA. . . . Justin would understand. I hear
his new book is all about Aspects of Truth.

REVEREND. Oh, dear, dear! (*Impatiently*)

HONORA. Well then, I've discovered myself; and
in a very different way. And my discovery is a
longing—a *longing* for Truth; in things big and
little. Yes, it's a commonplace. And yet, when I be-
gan to look about me, I could see very few things
in the world that were not boring and ugly,—when
they might be beautiful. If you looked at things
for yourself, and if you said what you meant, at
least you could never be bored. But people say so
glibly all the time, what they don't mean. Now,
look at the word "Obey" in your own marriage-
service.

REVEREND. Ah, ah! At last. Now we have it.
(*Beaming with relief and condescension*) A very
common objection, my dear girl. And as trifling as
it is unreasonable. Ah, this modern self-seeking!—
Admit, Honora, that a house must have a Head.

HONORA. (*Kindly*) If you like. Indeed, why
not?

REVEREND. You see, of course, that a House
cannot have two Heads.

HONORA. Why, no, Reverend, I don't see that, of
course, at all. There was Cerberus with three; and
the Hydra, you know, with any number of heads.
I'm sure they found uses for them all. Indeed there

are times, don't you truly think now, when one feels oneself, rather short of heads?

REVEREND. Er—er—my dear, this is trifling.

HONORA. Solemn earnest.—"*Obey*" in such a relation, at this age of this Planet! To put such a moral indignity upon the free, all-giving service of —of love!

REVEREND. FREE LOVE!!

HONORA. Heavens, No! Reverend, what are you thinking of? (*Incensed*)

REVEREND. (*Incensed*) I, thinking of! (JUSTIN *starts to re-enter and turns away laughing*) Oh, dear me.

HONORA. You know very well what I mean, if you will let yourself look at it fairly.

REVEREND. *I let myself*——!

HONORA. (*Earnestly*) You *know* that Self-sacrifice is the essence of woman's nature, when she's natural. What is obedience beside that?

REVEREND. My dear Honora, you picture an ideal state of things.

HONORA. Yes; why not?

REVEREND. Ah,—But.

HONORA. (*Coaxingly*) Ah, now, don't " But ". Once in a while, you see, somebody *wants* to be ideal; and then the whole world is astonished.—*I* would like to be . . . ideal.

REVEREND. But as society is now constituted, it has to be safe-guarded against——

HONORA. Everything it doesn't live up to! That's why it cannot grow. But religion, Reverend dear, hasn't such stupid things to do. It has to up-hold nothing but the truest, the deepest, the most beautiful!—Oh, Reverend,—and you're sitting on my Hat!

REVEREND. Er—Justin! Er——

HONORA. Justin, come back, do! Come and help him if you can. Oh, Justin. He is saying that two

Heads are better than one! (*Re-enter* JUSTIN, C.)
Eh, Reverend?

REVEREND. Honora, where did you learn all this,
about Love?

HONORA. Where indeed?

REVEREND. There is someone else—besides
Walter.

HONORA. (*After a pause*) Well, I do hope so!
(*Shaking her head with a sigh*)

REVEREND. You care for someone else.

HONORA. Not I! And I did so want to *love*
somebody. And I don't.

REVEREND. Then you never really cared for Wat.

HONORA. (*Honestly*) No. Not at all. But I
am somehow so impersonal; Walter didn't seem to
matter.

REVEREND. (*Groaning*) Impersonal!

HONORA. Now how hard you are to please.

REVEREND. Are you a woman at all?

HONORA. (*Meekly*) I don't know. I think so,
at least,—I never can write a letter without adding
one or two postscripts, if that's convincing. But I
suppose I must be a New Woman. You may have
me transfixed with a hat-pin, if you think it's best.
Or—or Justin will put me in a Book.

JUSTIN. I will.

(REVEREND *rises*.)

HONORA. Thank you for coming to talk it over.
(*Gives him her hand*) It's no earthly good, to be
honest, but I'll think over all the wise things you've
said.

REVEREND. Oh, *I* have said nothing, absolutely
nothing; if you recall the circumstance.

HONORA. (*Reproachfully*) Oh, Reverend! And
when I have (*going up center*) trusted you—with
my whole—Hat. (*Taking it from his nerveless*

fingers) But what *were* you going to say then?
You shall have the last word.

REVEREND. Ah!

HONORA. What then?

REVEREND. You freely offer *me*—the last word?

HONORA. Solemn earnest. What is it?

REVEREND. You are the Newest of New Women.
(*Benignly*)   There, there, keep it yourself, my
child, for your honesty.

HONORA. What?

REVEREND. (*Up stage*)   The last word! (*Exit
c. by the garden-door*)

(JUSTIN'S *pipe is conspicuously lightless.* HONORA
    *arranges her hat on the head of Hermes, and
    turns to him.*)

HONORA. You see? All this talk about Love and
Marriage!   And nobody will stand still and find
out, in the first place, what you are like, to love you
or not. Ah, well, of course, I have been most in-
considerate. But it won't hurt Walter, after this
week or two of duck-shooting. Did you see him before he left?

JUSTIN. Yes, last night.

HONORA. And did he look blighted?

JUSTIN. Candidly, no. After all, he is still something of an unlicked cub. You have your eyes
open; he has not. I don't understand how it ever
went so far,—for you.

HONORA. Neither do I. I don't suppose I can
make it clear to you. I sound sillier and sillier.
(*Comes down*)

JUSTIN. Please remember how much I am concerned with Aspects of Truth. As much concerned
as you. Let us dig up some now. (*Invitingly, he
pushes out a chair. She sits on the edge of it, with
sudden seriousness.* JUSTIN *takes one opposite and*

listens, with an occasional resort to his smokeless pipe) I used to hear of you when he was still in college.

HONORA. Oh yes, long ago.

JUSTIN. And when he went abroad?

HONORA. I wrote to him. (*She digs patterns with her parasol on the floor earnestly*)

JUSTIN. And when he came back?

HONORA. You see, it was horribly dull down here, there wasn't a human creature to relieve the landscape! Not satisfactorily human. And it used to come over me, how impossible it must be to know one's self ever, unless one can love somebody, some-day. And then, just then, Walter came back, and I was so glad to see him! I would have loved any-body,—anybody; without stopping to look. And so it was with Walter.

JUSTIN. The landscape required somebody.

HONORA. And I—tried—to make—him—" *do.*" —It's the *Truth.*

JUSTIN. I honor you for telling it.

HONORA. I thank you—for understanding; if— if you do.

JUSTIN. I do.

HONORA. You see?

JUSTIN. Yes. You are the first woman I ever saw.

HONORA. Ah, I'm so glad someone understands. And I've *said* it, and now . . . I'll take my book, and I'll take my hat . . . (*Disengaging it from the head of Hermes*)

JUSTIN. (*Rapt*) Yes, do! I mean—er—put it on. I—only wanted to—er—see it on. (R. *front*)

HONORA. What?

JUSTIN. Your Hat.

HONORA. (*Open-mouthed*) On what?

JUSTIN. On you;—your head, you know. You seem to prefer chairs and parasols and all manner of still-life. Ah!—(HONORA *puts on her hat, with-out trying it, and looks at him inquiringly*) We—we were wondering—before you came—what those long streamers were for, down behind——

HONORA.   Those are strings, to tie the Hat on.

JUSTIN.   Most provident.

HONORA.   Otherwise, you see, it would come off, easily.

JUSTIN.   And what was that you said about some Book?

HONORA.   Oh, *my* book! It's in the right-hand cupboard there. (*Pointing to the cabinet up* R. *of fireplace*)

JUSTIN.   You are writing a Book? (*Goes up to cupboard*)

HONORA.   Yes, I was. I mean I am. No, let me find it. Yours is a *real* book.

JUSTIN.   And it's in the left-hand cupboard! I locked it there last night. But, *your* Book—?

HONORA.   Oh, it's nothing but a Novel. (*Goes down* L.)

JUSTIN.   Nothing but!—The name—the name—what's it about?

HONORA.   It's about—yes, I'll tell you. It's about—Truth! Aspects of Truth! But I call it,—The Chameleon! (*Gleefully*) You know why. Because you think you have it, and you haven't. Because it changes color all day long. Because, now it's green and lovely; and then it's gray and ugly; and then it's rainbow; and then it's piebald. And it's so hard to catch and keep, and know what color it is. The Chameleon,—the Chameleon! Truth, the Chameleon.

JUSTIN.   And you were writing,—here, all these days?

HONORA.   Yes,—and I suppose it's true that I was writing myself into a state of mind, and out of it again. But I've begun to grow up! and I can only cling to my bean-stalk and see where it takes me. So—I'll just take my hat and my Book, and begone.

JUSTIN. Wait. Let me see the Book.

HONORA. Oh, no one has seen anything of it but Mr. Carrick.

JUSTIN. Quentin Carrick? Hm. But he knows something of style. Do you like Carrick?

HONORA. He's charming—on paper. (*Goes toward cupboard*)

JUSTIN. You shall leave the Book. (*Stopping her way to the cupboard*) And you shall go on writing here.

HONORA. Here? After all this?—Ah, I believe you *are* a philosopher, a real one.

JUSTIN. Why not? I heard you say just now that you wanted yourself to be a something ideal. Now I——

HONORA. Yes? You?—

JUSTIN. An I for an I!—All these good home people believe that an idealist is a man who goes to sea in a bowl. I'm simply trying——

HONORA. Yes——

JUSTIN. To find out——

HONORA. Yes——

JUSTIN. How to begin——

HONORA. Go on—go on!

JUSTIN. To be Real.

HONORA. (*Rapturously*) Ah . . . But I ought to go. Good-bye, and thank you. (*Going, she turns back*) And don't forget, when you are writing about Truth, that wretched world-old phrase, " too good to be true; "—it's a perfect *worm*. We shall find out some day, that all our " hateful " truths were hateful only because they were not true enough. Some day it will be all beautiful. It's so hard to find the *beginning. If only—we could ever begin at the beginning!* (*Going*)

JUSTIN. Come back! (HONORA *turns to look at him*) You were going without your hat;—I mean your Book.

HONORA. Oh!

JUSTIN. No, it has nothing to do with your Book. (*Facing her with determination*) Here is a chance for something to begin from the beginning.

HONORA. What?

JUSTIN. You:—and the Truth.

HONORA. You don't ask me to marry Walter? Now?

JUSTIN. No. I ask you . . .

HONORA. What then?

JUSTIN. To marry me. (*She backs away and stands looking at him with concern*) I haven't lost my wits. Don't be frightened away. You asked me to listen while you told your perplexities, poor child. I listened, and underneath your words, I heard my own heart talking. Yes, my heart. I knew I must have one. (*Smiling*) Your discovery was mine; your efforts were mine. And you, poor Truth, so young and green and valorous! You were like some dream of mine that took on a human likeness and faced me here. And I never could have uttered this wild thing to anyone else. It happens, because you are you, and I am I.

HONORA. (*Dazedly*) Because I am I . . .

JUSTIN. Yes.—Did you not say just now that we blame Truth for coming late? But we ourselves never begin at the beginning? And that people must always speak of things " too good to be true? " You seem to me too good to be true. But I know you are true. And I dare to tell you now. I'm going to begin at the very beginning. (*She looks at him with wide eyes and growing fascination*) Oh, it seems crazy, no doubt. But one thing is certain. I could not have begun much sooner; could I? (*She laughs nervously*) Truth is the one adventure: You know that. And you must share it with me. Truth, from the beginning—From the moment that I saw you, I knew that you were She —Your hunger, child; for you were hunghy. (*She nods*) Your loneliness; for you were lonely, weren't you? (*She nods*) Do you know that your face turned towards me, three times while you were talking? (*She shakes her head*) And you were right. If you will only trust me, as I trust you, you shall never be alone in the world again. (*Sounds from the house-door.* HONORA *starts out of her spell*)

HONORA. Oh, there is somebody! (*Takes flight c. to the garden*)

(*Enter* L., RUFUS, *hastily.*)

RUFUS. Hello, has Sylvester gone?

JUSTIN. Yes.

RUFUS. And what's the upshot of it all? (*Sits on table*) Will she,—won't she?

JUSTIN. She won't marry him.

RUFUS. (*Chuckling*) Poor Wat! To think Honora should break up a happy household like this!

(*Enter* ROSE L.)

ROSE. You might have waited to tell me what they said.

JUSTIN. Ah, you must ask Sylvester.

ROSE. But will she?

RUFUS. No, she won't. And after all she's much too clever for Wat, if he is my brother. Cheer up. You've always been so chummy with Honora. Everything will be just the same.

ROSE. (*Coming down* c., *tragically*)—How like a man! There *is* a grave side to the matter, Rufus.

It's one thing for a Writer—excuse me, Justin,—a Writer of Books to set people all examining their minds in this modern unwholesome way. Because they simply cannot write any kind of book without analyzing something,—

RUFUS. If it's only a Cook-book!

ROSE. They Write. But it is we who Live——

RUFUS. And Eat.

ROSE. And to us, who are Living——

RUFUS. Or eating——

ROSE. It's a very different matter. Honora has not only broken a happy and suitable engagement; but she has walked off in high feather, to finish her novel. The book's the thing! It always was. And it matters nothing to her that she has set everyone else self-searching and hair-splitting about the matter of Truth,—Truth—in all things, from the very beginning. And here is Justin who seems to sympathize with her.

JUSTIN. I do!

RUFUS. By Jove!

JUSTIN. And I have begged her to go on writing here every morning, all summer—er—in the corner somewhere. It's so cool and quiet.

ROSE. But you! Your Book.

JUSTIN. I won't let her disturb me.—My book's done,—or very nearly. Come. I've heard you talking Honora for years. Do stand by her, now.

ROSE. Well, you are brotherly!

JUSTIN. Heaven forbid!

ROSE. Oh, then you wouldn't like her for a sister of your own, on second thought.

JUSTIN. (*Judicially*) No. Perhaps not: on second thought. But I'm immensely interested in her Book.

ROSE. Well, of all the cold-blooded things I have ever seen, there is nothing to equal a man of letters! Honora is positively charming; if you took the trouble to look at her. I give you up. Rufus, come. We are interrupting him; and I know you'll both talk if I go away; and I want to hear.

(*Exeunt* ROSE *and* RUFUS L. *to the house.* JUSTIN *watches them out, smiling; then turns expectantly* C. HONORA *appears up* C. *and re-enters. She has a shy and younger air.*)

JUSTIN. Ah!—Again, you've come true. You left—your Book?

HONORA. Yes, but I did not come for that. I came, because—I wanted—to hear more. (*Coming down a step or two*)

JUSTIN. You *wanted* to hear more!

HONORA. Yes.

JUSTIN. (*Rapturously*) Ah, don't you see? We two have more to give each other than any man and woman on the planet?—If you are not afraid to be " fantastic ".

HONORA. Ah! (*Drawing nearer*)

JUSTIN. And we have only to make one solemn compact—To tell each other the *absolute* truth—in all things; at all times; on demand.

HONORA. But others *could* do that.

JUSTIN. Indeed they could! But they seem not to know it. They never learn. They are bound to live on saw-dust, and die of boredom!—When they might explore the stars. (*Radiantly*)

HONORA. But—but of course—I don't love you, Justin.

JUSTIN. How can you be sure you don't? You've only seen me some twenty-five minutes. Now the moment I saw *you,* (*Solemnly*) I knew that you were She. I knew. So, even if you did not know that I was He——

HONORA. What then?

JUSTIN. I must be He, you know. There isn't anybody else for me to be. (*He takes her hands firmly and looks at her*) Honora, I am He.

HONORA. I—I must go.

JUSTIN. (*Letting her hands go, and standing away a little*) You are coming back; every morning, all the summer, till your Book's done, and my Book's done, and we are both wise enough to say a thing or two to this generation! Yes, wise enough to look the old world through the eyes and say "*Good-Morning*"!— Will you?

HONORA. Y—n–n–n—Yes!

JUSTIN. And you accept what I tell you?

HONORA. N—nn—Yes!

JUSTIN. You are She; and I am He. And you shall walk up and down and round and round my heart until you know us both, completely. It's a pledge. I am yours, Honora, whether you are mine, or not. But you are coming true.　. . .

HONORA. What would they——

JUSTIN. No one will know. They couldn't understand yet. What do they know of Life? Who never dream? You're coming true, Honora?

HONORA. (*Firmly*) Yes. Good-bye. (*Goes; turns and comes back*) Justin——

JUSTIN. Honora!

HONORA. I just remembered. I—it wasn't . . . it wasn't *quite* true about——

JUSTIN. Oh, you eighth Wonder! About what?

HONORA. Those hat-strings. The Hat wouldn't really come off at all, you know, without;—save in a high wind. They are often in the way. But I wear them; because I think they—I thought they were—more becoming. (*Starting back a little*) Are they?

JUSTIN. (*Earnestly*) *Yes.*

HONORA. (*Starting back a little*) Good-bye! (*Going, she returns slowly*) Oh, one thing more.

Justin—I—it was not entirely true, this last thing I said, about the Hat-strings. I mean, I didn't really come back to tell you that. I really came—to tell you . . .

JUSTIN. Tell me!—

HONORA. (*Backing away from him by degrees, with a shining face*) All that you say—is wonderful to me. . . . It makes me—almost—Love you!

(*She runs away through the garden.*)

CURTAIN.

ACT II.

SCENE:—*The same; three months later. Autumn afternoon. There is now a tall cuckoo-clock on the house stairway. The garden door is closed. There are autumn flowers about. HONORA'S hat adorns the head of Hermes L. C. L. down, at a paper-strewn table, HONORA. R. down, at another table, JUSTIN. Between them, down C. the Japanese screen half-folded back. They are both abstracted; HONORA playing with her pen nervously; JUSTIN gazing at her like a visionary. HONORA seizes her pen, poises it ominously, and writes something with an air of finality and determination; then puts down her pen.*)

JUSTIN. At last!—*The End. And now*—(*He rises jubilantly. Knock at the house-door*)

(ROSE *appears there.*)

ROSE. I know I'm interrupting. But you've written as long as it's good for you to.

JUSTIN. My dear, we're horribly busy.

ROSE. I *must* talk to somebody.

JUSTIN. Wait a bit, do. I was entirely wrapped up—(*Exit* ROSE *impatiently*) star-gazing;—at Honora.

HONORA. You moved it.

JUSTIN. What?

HONORA. The screen.

JUSTIN. Place was growing as bleak as a barn.

HONORA. This warm day!

JUSTIN. I couldn't see you. Does it bother you, really? (*He crosses; and folds the screen round her chair completely*) There you are, Truth, at the bottom of the well.

HONORA. (*Hidden*) Hé—

JUSTIN. Out of sight and out of mind! Do you see any stars down there?

HONORA. Oh!

JUSTIN. Nobody knows you and nobody cares. You're the unwelcome Truth: do you hear? And whenever you show your disagreeable face, you crack an illusion!

HONORA. Justin,—Justin Aurelius, help!

JUSTIN. What will you give me, Truth, if I let you out?

HONORA. Ah!

JUSTIN. The time is up—Have I kept all my promises? Have I been good?

HONORA. Yes.

JUSTIN. Have I loved you far off—enough?

HONORA. Yes.

JUSTIN. Then stand forth—Dearest. Show yourself—to the world and me! (*He lifts away the screen suddenly and surprises her with her hands over her eyes*) Honora!—Tears?

HONORA. (*Laughing nervously*) Oh, nothing, nothing! I— You see—it was so dark down in the well! (*He holds out his arms*) Oh, not yet!

(*Knock on the garden door. Enter* c., RUFUS, *pipe in hand.*)

RUFUS. I say, I want to— What's the matter with the screen?

JUSTIN. My dear fellow, we're awfully hard at work. And I find my presence disturbs Honora. She's absorbed in her last chapter.

RUFUS. By Jove, Honora, is it a bad ending? Don't! I'm a perfect child about bad endings.— I'll go.— Thought your working hours were over.

JUSTIN. Not to-day, though. See you soon: if you don't mind. (*Returns to his table with a desperate air of business, taking the screen after him and setting it up before his own table. Exit* RUFUS)

(HONORA *rises and crosses* R., *knocks on the screen as if it were a door.*)

HONORA. (*Meekly*) Justin.

JUSTIN. Is it Truth?

HONORA. No. Nothing but Honora.

JUSTIN. Nothing But!—(*Pushes aside the screen and gently takes her hands. He kisses them: and looks at her gladly*) Nothing But!— Tell me. It's really done   ?

HONORA. Yes . . . But yours? (*He points to the left-hand cupboard happily*) How beautiful it is!

JUSTIN. Where you touched it.

HONORA. I have done nothing but delay it.

JUSTIN. You did that. For I had to write it all over again; all over again in the light of you.— Ah—(*Cuckoo-clock chirrups four*) Oh, be quiet. (*To* HONORA) Do you really find it beautiful, you?

HONORA. The whole world will find it beautiful. And so brave.

JUSTIN. Brave?

HONORA. Yes. Because it is simple: or sounds so. You've been great enough to say wise things simply. It is all as limpid——

JUSTIN. But that's all you! If anything had shaken my faith in you, there would have been no more Book.

HONORA. Do you mean that? (*He smiles at her*) Yes, yes. Of course I know you mean it. But it's too much.

JUSTIN. Then let us talk of *your* Book. For I know it, all but the ending. And how beautiful it is! What a marvellous *Chameleon*,—a rainbow beast! Ah, you'll know some day how proud I am of you. And Carrick says . . . Do you know why I'm never jealous of Carrick? He isn't a man; He's a Book. But now!— Summer's over; the books are done.— Life begins. . . . Was I selfish to ask it, when I've had you to look at, all these mornings? And when I've heard you say . . . . that you love me—that you do, you do love me?

HONORA. To ask——?

JUSTIN. At the end of the summer——

HONORA. You mean?——

JUSTIN. My kiss . . .

HONORA. (*Shrinking a little*) I—I—all the time—(*A knock*) I was——

JUSTIN. Yes—(*A knock*) You were——?

HONORA. (*Hurriedly*) I was—saving it!

(*Enter* C., WALTER, *with a shot-gun and a cloth wherewith to polish it.* JUSTIN *impatient.*)

WALTER. I say, you two have worked long enough. It's after four.

JUSTIN. It's the last day.

WALTER. Well, and it takes the last trump to make any impression upon your hearing. 'Ought to beg pardon, may-be. But you see Rose is out there, in tears.

JUSTIN. Rose?

HONORA. What now?

WALTLR. 'M-hm— Crying on the verandah—Says you have finished your books and her happiness together; with a single *Finis*, as it were. There's an indictment for you. That's what comes of being Literary!-- Came in for a home-thrust myself. She told me that if you, Nora, had not discovered that you were far too clever for me, you never would have——

JUSTIN. Oh, come, come!

HONORA. Wat, how shabby of you!

WALTER. M-hm. She did. And I told her, Nora, that you were quite right; and that I had come to—sight—it (*Looking along his gun-barrel carefully*) precisely as you do. But it did not cheer her. This dissatisfaction of hers with Rufus seems to have blamed little to do with Rufus!--- It's very modern. So you'd better let her in, and find out what you've been up to. (*Exit* JUSTIN) You probably don't know.-- Literary People are so absent-minded. You are like Rousseau stirring up the French Revolution; you are like the shilling shockers that lure small boys to run away, and play Pirate. Rose--is playing pirate. (*Still he polishes*) Now murder is all very well in its way, and even necessary . . . at times. But when it comes to the choice of guests she has made for to-morrow night! I wish she wouldn't be so unscrupulous.

HONORA. Oh, that dinner?

WALTER. Of course, *I* am good-looking: and "*you* have your Mind," as Rose says. And we'll be there.-- But then there's the Reverend, and Aunt Eunice.

HONORA. Really?

WALTER. And Kilmayne, that old sport!

HONORA. She hadn't seen him for years.

WALTER. Why ask him?

HONORA. Auld acquaintance?

WALTER. —There is, now and then, an "auld acquaintance" that should be forgot, distinctly. Then, Mrs. Van Wyck! Oh, wait till you see Mrs. Van Wyck.—I tell you, it's going to be a feast of Nero, with all of us living torches.— And Thomas is coming, Nora, James Roberts Thomas.

HONORA. Oh, Wat! Don't tell me that.

WALTER. I thought you liked him. You ought to. He's *Literary*.

HONORA. Ugh!

WALTER. He is, though.

HONORA. (*Simulating the gushing hostess*) "*So-and-so*" you'll be so drawn to *Who's this!*— You both carry umbrellas, I know, in bad weather!

WALTER. Come now, he has been chasing you about, to read that thesis of his, as it were one bitten by a gad-fly.

HONORA. Oh, that thesis! (*She begins to clear up her papers*)

WALTER. Must be deep, you know. He read me a page of it, and I couldn't make head or tail of the thing; so I referred him to you.

HONORA. Ah, Wat!—I have put off hearing that thesis for eight weeks, upon a hundred excuses.

WALTER. Ah, Truth!

HONORA. All based upon three excellent reasons: I don't want to: I don't want to: I don't w-ant to!

(WALTER *picks up a card from the table and reads.*)

WALTER. Carrick. Hm—hm——

HONORA. But surely he can't read his thesis to me to-morrow night? At dinner?

WALTER. Oh, can't he? You don't know him.—
Never mind, Nora. At least, he shan't take you
out. You shall have Carrick. And *he's* Literary.
Why you like him I. don't know. But he's plainly
interested in *you,* as far as a man of letters can be
—now-a-days. Once upon a time literary people
fell in love; or said they did: and wrote about it
What comes over the young man's fancy, I wonder? Look at Justin, now. He writing in one window; and you in the other all summer! And by the
year after next it will dawn upon him that he might
have been making love to you, a few days at least—
Spite of that, though, I'm not half ashamed of him.
In a crowd of lions, you'd take him for a man—I
even like the stuff he writes— And I'm nothing if
not severe.

HONORA. I know. (*Crosses* R., *with her MSS.
and locks them in the right-hand cabinet, lingeringly*)

WALTER. Won't it be funny to try for a plain
unbiased opinion of yours when it's out? I suppose it will knock everything flat.— You have such
a way of saying Nothing so fetchingly. I'm told
that indicates Style. And it is seldom seen in English.

HONORA. Who told you that?

WALTER. Your loving Publisher. Met him in
town yesterday. Wish I'd asked him to join the
procession of animals to-morrow night. He told
me—that if the ending is up to the rest of it, it will
be—(steady, now!) The Book of the Season.
Yes,—*The Chameleon:* Book of the Season!— He
was struck with your graphic insight into the Modern Man.—I say, Nora, did you dig all that out of
Carrick, or me? Or do I furnish just the superficial element that's going to make it sell? Poor
Wat! By the way, Nora, you'll find my perfect
portrait in the works of William Shakespere—if

you Literary people ever read him. Yes, you will
though; here it is. (*Going to book-case and pull-
ing out a volume. He declaims cheerfully, till he
finds the place*) " By this, *poor Wat,* far off, upon
a hill " . . . Here we are! " Stands on his hinder
legs, with listening ear!" What a picture. Poor
Wat!—(*The house door opens*) Here's Rose.
And she is going to tell you " precisely " what she
means; if you think you can " catch the idea!"
(*Exit* c., *hastily*)

(*Re-enter* L., JUSTIN, *with* ROSE *who is filled with
tragic importance.*)

HONORA. Rose, dear, is it anything new? Wat
tells me there is something wrong with you.

ROSE. I tried to tell you before now. But you
were writing away, both of you, oblivious of all real
life;—writing, like Bats!

JUSTIN. You may call me a Bat or anything else
you choose, sis. But what's it all about? Surely
you and Rufus——

ROSE. In a word: we have decided upon a legal
separation.

JUSTIN. Eh?

HONORA. No, no!

ROSE. Yes. We have agreed.— That is, I have.

HONORA. Oh, Rose, Rose! How mistaken.
How preposterous.

ROSE. You call *me* mistaken!—and if it had not
been for you—and Justin too!—digging after the
foundations of Truth in everything, we might have
lived on in perfect comfort:——

HONORA. Rose!

ROSE. Utterly unsuited as we are.

HONORA. Rose!

ROSE. Can you suppose that you two are monop-
olists of the search for the Ideal?

JUSTIN. Rose!

ROSE. That you are a Truth Trust? . . . You write. But it is we who Live! For you it may be all most painless and lovely theorizing, with your One adventure of Truth in all things great and small. But it remained for us to practise what you talk about, for us to live it. And so I found out——

JUSTIN. Well?

ROSE. (*Weeping*) That Rufus——

JUSTIN. Yes, yes?

ROSE. Was really in love with someone else——

JUSTIN. ⎫
⎬ He is?
HONORA. ⎭

ROSE. Not *now*, of course! (*Indignantly*) *Was* when he married me.

HONORA. ⎫
⎬ He told you that?
JUSTIN. ⎭

ROSE. He thought I would like it! It was the Truth.— The hideous truth. It means that I was a second thought: that—in that vulgar phrase—I was caught on the rebound! *I* was—*I* was!

JUSTIN. He up and told you that out of a clear sky? He's a brute.

ROSE. He is not a brute. He was blindly following your lead:—and mine.

JUSTIN. Yours?

ROSE. Of course he knew I was not—wildly in love with him, when I married him. But I was very young. It took me longer to grow up than it takes most girls. Of course I *was* fond of him. But I was full of idealism—(JUSTIN *and* HONORA *look at each other incredulously*) the hero-worship of a very young girl. If you understand what I mean.— And Rufus has no idealism in his nature.

JUSTIN. Mm.— Did you worship some hero when you married Rufus?

ROSE. There was someone I—I knew—very slightly.

JUSTIN. Ah!

ROSE. But he affected my imagination in a way that you two can hardly understand. If you ever fall in love,—you will learn how much it has to do with unreachable ideals. I used to see him ride by the house; and once I danced with him, somewhere.

JUSTIN. Ah. And he said——?

ROSE. Oh, almost nothing. The merest nothings. But you'll find out, when once you begin to Live, how little there is in Words.

JUSTIN. By Jove! Then it was rebound with Rufus, too.

ROSE. That is a very different matter with a young girl, too young to understand herself.— And I never saw him again:—after that dance.

HONORA. He—he died?

ROSE. No.

HONORA. What did he do?

ROSE. How do I know? Aren't you two always saying that it isn't what one does; it's what one *Is?*— But when it comes to practise——

JUSTIN. Ah! And you are ready to give up all that's in your hands for this dream out of ancient history?

ROSE. Aren't you both always saying that one must begin with the very beginning?

HONORA. Ah!

ROSE. (*Darkly*) Yes. And in Real Life, Justin, we go further. (*Impressively*) *I* will go further. If the Beginning is not apparent, I am ready to Dig it Up!

JUSTIN. But surely Rufus doesn't care a jackstraw about the other woman now.

ROSE. He shall have opportunity to decide.

HONORA. How?

JUSTIN. For the love of heaven!

ROSE. You will see her to-morrow night.

JUSTIN. Not Aunt Eunice!

HONORA. Mrs. Van Wyck!

ROSE. Mrs. Van Wyck. We have talked it all over;—quite as dispassionately as if *we* were Literary. And I hope that you may both learn—painlessly—something from our experience.—Mrs. Van Wyck is a widow.

HONORA. And—your hero?

ROSE. It seems—Rufus heard—he's visiting the Reverend. We've asked them both. (*Moved to tears*)

JUSTIN. Who is he? Who the devil? Not Carrick! He *never* says nothing.

ROSE. Rufus told me so much about that woman's charming laugh! I rely on you to—keep her laughing all through dinner-time. And I hear, she sings!

JUSTIN. What about Him? Be fair. What can he do that's irresistible? Ride—ride!—Shall we make him ride? And if so, where?

ROSE. How like a man.—But Rufus, at least, did catch my idea. We are not going to hold each other to a bond that does not satisfy the highest demands of our natures.— We are going to be truthful, from *the beginning:* and as generous as we can. There shall be no reproaches. (*With lofty pity*) In Real Life, Justin,—people Do things.— If that woman with the laugh still charms him, he shall marry her, (*sobbing*) if she were a laughing hy—hy—hyena!

JUSTIN. But who's the man?

HONORA. Major Kilmayne!—Oh, Rose, Rose!—And here comes Mr. Carrick through the garden.—

(ROSE *starts up and dries her eyes.*)

ROSE. That man again!— Do be composed, all of you. I'll come back when I'm fit to behold. (*Starting away, she turns, at the foot of the house-steps and says with a fluttered air*) I—I—you may think me very self-conscious; but it does seem to me that he comes here almost too often. (*Exit* L.)

JUSTIN. (*Hurriedly*) I won't have her black-guarding you like this, as a destroyer of public peace. Let her take me for a frozen ink-well!— Come, tell her, dearest,—tell her you are going to be mine.— Give her another idea:—suggestion, suggestion,—hypnosis!— She'll come back with an olive-branch in her beak.

HONORA. Oh, Justin, not yet! Don't tell her!— Some day I will—if I must. Not yet.——

JUSTIN. Soon, then. Ah, can't we be married soon? (CARRICK *appears* C., *outside*) Oh, confound him!

HONORA. Go and soothe her feelings if you can. But don't tell—yet.

(*Exit* JUSTIN L., *into the house.* CARRICK *knocks at the door* C. HONORA *goes and opens it slowly, disappearing behind it, at the same time, while she holds the knob.*)

CARRICK. (*Inquiringly*) Good-afternoon.

(*He is a faultlessly dressed man, between forty and fifty; a literary man of the world, with a carefully impassive, pale face, that lights up once in a while with curious interest. He stands on the threshold and waits for* HONORA *to re-appear.*)

HONORA. (*Emerging, slowly*) Good-afternoon to you.

CARRICK. (*Blandly*) Why do you hide? You look rather like the dweller in a glass-house, waiting to throw stones.

HONORA. (*Hastily*) Oh!

CARRICK. Dare I come in?

HONORA. (*Recovering herself*) Come in, come in! Work is over; and well over.

CARRICK. The Book is done?—I cangratulate you.— And Hopefar's Book, of course.

HONORA. Oh yes, that's done, too.

CARRICK. Do we congratulate Hopefar?

HONORA. We do. It is indeed a Book! But You don't know it, yet.

CARRICK. No. You do.

HONORA. Oh, yes. He says . . . in fact . . . I—I shall be proud to have had a hand in that book.

CARRICK. (*Looking about*) I haven't seen you here for some time, without that good Argus pretending to ply his quill.

HONORA. Pretending?

CARRICK. My child! . . . Candidly, when is this game of truth to end? It ought to reach a climax now: since the Books are done. Unless Hopefar persuades you to rewrite the last chapter. (*Watching her*)

HONORA. Oh, he did!

CARRICK. The devil he did!

HONORA. (*Glibly*) I've been re-writing it these five days. Now, it's done.

CARRICK. (*Lighting a cigarette*) May I? Thanks. As one of the sponsors of your work, allow me to remark, you are a woman of the most extraordinary temperament.

HONORA. Ah! " Temperament!"— Br–r. (*Shrugging her shoulders*)

CARRICK. I'm awfully grateful to you. You set me guessing-- How you're going to dispose of Hopefar.

HONORA. (*Nervously*) Why should I have to dispose of him?— Dear me! Haven't you heard Rose's complaints that I'm wasted on the library air?— Eh? They who Live; and we that Write!

CARRICK. Yes . . . You see, I write, myself. I know something about the point of view.

HONORA. (*Rallying*) Not Justin's!

CARRICK. Hm!—(*Looks at the table, down* R. *and sits there, looking at her*) Let's try Justin's point of view. Really,—not half bad. (*She makes an impatient gesture*) Don't apologize. The first time I ever saw you, I had a singular curiosity to see you—angry. Yes, really, I believe you're almost capable of a rage. And it's a very rare gift, you know,—in these good old Peace-Conference times. I'm sure you could hate somebody if you tried. It's a lost art. Loving is a much more obvious virtue. Though one could never expect you to love, like an ordinary woman. You have too much temperament. Er—I beg you—don't lose it.

HONORA. How should I lose it? (*She stands facing him*)

CARRICK. Ah, well!— You see; if it were not an easy word to abuse, I should almost say you have a complicating streak of genius. But from Justin's point of view—and it's a very comfortable one—you look—er—almost appealingly Feminine. Just that; nothing more.

HONORA. Well? (*She has started half-angrily from her former attitude*)

CARRICK. What Justin is like, from *your* point of view,—he doesn't know.

HONORA. (*Calmly*) Do you?

CARRICK. Brava! (*Laughing*) No matter. It's in your book that we shall all find Justin. (*He crosses and hands her the cigarettes*) Do. (*She hesitates and makes a negative gesture; then takes one and lights it, trying to be tranquil*) He'll be there. And I'm rather sorry fr Justin. He's a good fellow, mind you,—even if his ethical turn of mind is a bit—er—ridiculous. He might go into the book, you know,—unexpurgated.

HONORA. How do you know Justin is in the book?

CARRICK. My dear young lady!

HONORA. Not an explicit reply.

CARRICK. Pardon me, it is. For you are very young; and you understand so little of men.— Shall we play your game of Truth?

HONORA. Yes; if it's new to you.

CARRICK. Ah!— *The Chameleon* is turning dark.— You're almost angry. Don't apologize. It's something I wanted to see, you know. (HONORA *startled, coughs over her cigarette, throws it away pettishly; pulls a rose out of the flower bowl on the table, and eats it absent-mindedly, petal by petal*) Well, then. A statement and a piece of counsel all from your admiring servant.— The Book is full of Justin. For you were young and wise enough to know you knew nothing of men; you were charmingly foolish enough to suppose it had to be true: You wanted to dig it all out of some man's—er, heart. And Justin is the man to let you do it.

HONORA. Go on. It's very interesting.

CARRICK. Indeed, my—er, my dear young thing, it is uncommon interesting. I've regarded it, going on under my nose,—to be figurative—and I've marvelled at the greenness of our sage, Justin.

HONORA. Sage-green, maybe? Justin is not the Chameleon: that is certain. His hue is too unvaryingly—green.

CARRICK. He understands as little about women as any of us understand about—say, to preserve the unities,—Truth.

HONORA. Well?—I've been digging my novel out of Justin's mind and experience? Yes? And now? Next?

CARRICK. Oh, as to that, there's no earthly reason why you shouldn't dig your book out of Justin —or me—or any of us. Types are rare: individuals even rarer. And Justin is an individual. But— er—don't—*marry* Justin.

(HONORA *walks deliberately around her table once and then faces him, with sudden good humor, inscrutably.*)

HONORA. Why not?

CARRICK. (*With a chagrined laugh*) Brava!— The only woman I ever met who could argue. Why shouldn't you marry Justin? Why, you should, if you want to.— And it would be in keeping with your temperament to be able to want things— Only —you don't want to.

HONORA. "*The King of France with twenty thousand men!*"

CARRICK. And Justin will, of course, ask you to marry him. (*Relighting his cigarette*) Because—

HONORA. Because?

CARRICK. Justin is so prone to do the obvious thing. (Ah, the Chameleon grows resplendent.) Because he thinks he understands you from the beginning. He believes in one simple You. Whereas you are not a woman; but a mind; a Will, an eagerness; an illusion.— And you have a right to your own life; and experiments.

HONORA. Experiments?

CARRICK. Mark me. I'm quite serious. With your temperament and will-power, there are few things you could not do.

HONORA. (*With gay challenging*) Then I might even fall in love with Justin, if I tried?— Do you think I could?

CARRICK. (*Piqued*) Ah,—already . . . And you'll fool him to the end of the chapter.

HONORA. It's more than likely.— But how will the chapter end?

(*Enter from the house* L., REVEREND SYLVESTER *saying " Not at all, not at all!" and escorting* MRS. SHUTTLEWORTH, *stout, elderly, deaf and splendid,—followed by* JAMES ROBERTS THOMAS, Ph. D., *with a MS. under his arm,—* WALTER, RUFUS *and* ROSE.)

CARRICK. (*Half to himself*) Most timely enter of the leading heavy!

ROSE. We'll have our tea here, Nora. (I don't believe in letting them work too long) Here's Aunt Eunice,—and the Reverend—and Mr. James!

HONORA. You mean Roberts, dear.

THOMAS. I beg pardon,—Thomas. It *is* rather confusing. So happy to have caught you here, Miss Thorpe, at last. Walter told me you were to be found here almost every day; in the library.

HONORA. How very kind of you, Walter. (*Goes to the cup-board with her MSS.*)

(*The man,* THOMAS, *brings in the tea-things and places them down* R. *by* HONORA. ROSE, MRS. SHUTTLEWORTH *and the* REVEREND SYLVESTER *down* L. *The others about, partaking in both conversations.*)

THOMAS. And I greeted the opportunity, necessarily. I've called so often at your own house, and never had the good fortune to find you at hime.

HONORA. Oh! (*He unfolds a MS.*)

THOMAS. I want—yes, yes—hm,—perhaps after a little. But, it seems a bit noisy.

HONORA. Oh, don't think of it! It's far too noisy.

THOMAS. What a delightful woman, Mrs. Shuttleworth!— So extraordinarily appreciative for one of her years. I never met her before, you know. But I found her an enchanting listener. A rare gift, that, of listening gracefully. (*Turning over his MS.* HONORA *pours tea*)

REVEREND. (*To* MRS. SHUTTLEWORTH) And how are you, now-a-days, dear lady? The—ah— difficulty of the—ah——

MRS. SHUTTLEWORTH. (*Touching her ear*) It come and goes; it comes and goes. I left my fan in the carriage, I think. Ah, here comes Justin. (*Enter* JUSTIN *with her fan*) Here— Thank you. (*Holds her fan, later, between her teeth, to hear the better*) Tell me again, who's that young man talking to Honora.— He seems to be very full of information; of some kind. He talked to me uninterruptedly all the way, as we drove here, but I didn't catch a word.

(REVEREND *replies in her ear.*)

THOMAS. (R. *to* HONORA *over the tray*) Oh, thank you very much. Is this for me? But, I— er—if you please, no lemon thank you! Only a little hot water; and one lump. Oh, no Tea, if you please. Only a Little Hot Water; and One Lump, one Lump.— As I was saying, I have rarely met so keenly appreciative a—(*Observes* MRS. SHUTTLE-WORTH *and her Fan—the* REVEREND *shouting in her ear*) Oh, dear me, is it possible?

HONORA. I fear so.— And all your philosophy gone to waste; like attar of rose.

THOMAS. Oh, you're really too gracious.— A heavy trial this, of deafness;— Oh no, no cake, thank you; no cake, no cake! I never take sweets. Save, indeed, the one Lump with a little hot water.

(*Cuckoo-clock chirps five.*)

REVEREND. What a vivacious monitor! Surely it's new?

ROSE. There! I told them it was needed. I put it in two months ago. I had to insist. Before that, you see, I had to look in every few minutes to tell Justin what time it was. (I knew he would never stop to look at his watch.) One has to take such care of men of letters. And they are never grateful.

CARRICK. Ah, really, you know! (*Crossing* L.)

ROSE. So nice to see you. I found your card here, on the table this morning. So stupid of them not to send it to me. I was close by in the summerhouse.

MRS. SHUTTLEWORTH. (*Loudly*) Who is that horsey person you are asking to-morrow evening to meet us?

RUFUS. (*Quickly*) Kilmayne? Ah, you've met him? He's an old friend of Rose's, it seems. I don't know him.

ROSE. I used to know him—very slightly. And I thought it would be pleasant to ask him. He's stopping with the Reverend. He used to—to— to ride like a centaur!

MRS. SHUTTLEWORTH. A *centaur!* Most unpleasant idea. A centaur at the table.—I saw him this afternoon.

RUFUS. And can he talk?

MRS. SHUTTLEWORTH. If he can, I didn't hear him.

REVEREND. Oh, you may be sure it didn't signify at all. But he's a good fellow, Kilmayne: good family. Mother was a——

MRS. SHUTTLEWORTH. I insist that I don't want a centaur to take me out to dinner. Most unpleasant simile. As bad as a two-headed Girl.

REVEREND. (L.) Oh, when it comes to that, you know, there was Cerberus with three heads, and the

Hydra with any number of heads at all! I'm sure he found them all convenient.

HONORA. More tea, Reverend?

REVEREND. Er—thank you. With cream. (*Genially*) And, as to that, you know. I have sometimes found myself wishing that I had—er—*two heads.*

CARRICK. Never! Believe me,—you are almost, an ideal type, quite as you are.

REVEREND. "*Almost!*" Ah, but—(*Vivaciously*) to be confidential, I'd like to be ideal, myself; quite, quite Ideal. Why not, indeed? Why not? (*Cuckoo-clock*)

JUSTIN. (R. *to* HONORA) You look tired and *distraite.* What has anybody been saying to you?

HONORA. What indeed, but *Quack-quack! Baa-baa!*

JUSTIN. Poor Truth! I'll get them away as soon as I can. And then you'll tell me——

HONORA. *Quack-quack! Baa-baa!*

(REVEREND *draws near, stirring his tea.*)

JUSTIN. You need some tea. (*Pours some out for her*)

HONORA. I can't say anything else. I'm catching it.

JUSTIN. I'll break the spell. Here.——

HONORA. *Quack*——

THOMAS. (*Approaching*) You look as if you were saying something so interesting.

HONORA. (*Benignly*) *Quack!—Baa-baa.*

THOMAS. You're so irresistibly humorous. A rare gift now-a-days, that of true humor. I often resent the lack of it in others. As I say, somewhere in—let me see—(*Taking out his MS. again*) hm-hm,—yes, yes——

REVEREND. (L. *to* ROSE) Extraordinary thing, this hour of five o'clock. No matter how serious

one's vocation, talk always degenerates, most delightfully, into a kind of—I might almost say—er—
Quack-quack—Baa-baa!

Rose. How dear of you!——

Mrs. Shuttleworth. I didn't quite catch it.

Reverend. (*Embarrassed*) Well I—I——

Mrs. Shuttleworth. Surely I didn't understand you to say *Quack, quack!?*

Reverend. I—er——

Mrs. Shuttleworth. What is the point?——

Rufus. (*Interposing*) Tell us more about Kilmayne.

Reverend. Oh, but you'll see him to-morrow. So good of you to ask us. (*Rises.* Justin *speaks with him*)

Carrick. (R. *to* Honora) it's awfully *banal*, you know, to read the ending before you come to it. But one thing is clear, in the largest type.— You've made a magnificent fool of Justin.

(Mrs. Shuttleworth *rises to go.*)

Reverend. Not at all, not at all! Thomas and I will see you to your carriage.

Carrick. We will all see you to your carriage,— And I'll carry your fan, like Peter.

(*Exeunt all but* Justin *and* Rufus: Honora *last.*)

Justin. (*To* Honora) Come back. Come Back!

(*Exit* Honora l.)

Rufus. See here. Did you ever hear of a man who was angel-pecked? Well, I am. And I want a word with you about all this infernal nonsense.

Justin. Nonsense?

RUFUS. Yes. To-morrow night, the dinner; and the old sweethearts.

JUSTIN. What do *you* mean by it? Rose has just unburdened her mind. What was the origin of your untimely candor?

RUFUS. Untimely it was. As for the origin of it,—it's *Honora!* (*Explosively*) For a good-looking girl, with brains beside, she stirs up more trouble in the world!— That's just the row. Be brainy, if you like; but hideous. Or be good-looking if you can; and all is well.

JUSTIN. What has Honora got to do with it?

RUFUS. Honora has to do with everything that Rose does! Only Rose doesn't know it. Honora makes a pattern, of some fantasticality. And Rose cuts up everything she owns, in a fever of emulation, and tries to make it fit. There you are.

JUSTIN. But the widow! Mrs. Van Wyck?

RUFUS. The devil fly away with her!— Haven't seen her for years. Boy's first love; and all that. Laughed at a fellow's jokes. All wonder; (*Sketching on the air*) and bushy hair; and arched eyebrows, and "*Do tell me all about it! Precisely, what do you mean?*"— Had an awfully fetching laugh.—I say!— (*Firmly*) Yes, she did! When I heard she'd married somebody I was all broken up.

JUSTIN. You never asked her to marry you?

RUFUS. Certainly not. Nothing but a boy. I raked up all this to satisfy Rose's thirst for a perfect confidence. And as you might know, it's the first and last time I ever tell the truth, the whole truth and nothing but the truth.—Put *that* in a footnote of your "*Aspects of Truth.*" *I've* had enough of it!—As a matter of fact, she really does want to see that beggar, Kilmayne.

JUSTIN. Have no fear. He's a sport, and nothing more.

RUFUS. No accounting for women. They love extremes. Now I'm no extreme. I'm neither a sport, nor a man of letters.—It needn't have happened. I say it's too damned superfluous!—I'm thankful Honora's old book is done.—It ought to be illustrated with X-ray plates, and bound in human skin.

JUSTIN. Oh, come!

RUFUS. She has set the household by the ears;—wasted your time; stirred up trouble between Rose and me, put everything——

JUSTIN. Hold on!——

RUFUS. —Asunder;—thrown over one brother—

JUSTIN. She's going to marry—the other.

RUFUS. Who? What? How? Not me!

JUSTIN. She's going to marry me.

RUFUS. *You!* Honora?—My dear boy! I say —I never dreamed of it! (*Confounded*) All this time—(*Shaking hands madly*)

JUSTIN. Yes, hush. Not a word, yet, to anyone. Have your cannibal feast to-morrow night. Face your old sweethearts, and see how they look to you now. But don't blame this nonsense on Nora. She is the one soul of—Ah, here she comes!

(*Re-enter HONORA L. from house.*)

HONORA. Justin—I *must* speak to you. I have something to—(*Seeing RUFUS*) Oh! to-morrow, then. To-morrow! Another time. (*Going towards garden door*)

RUFUS. I say, wait a second,—Honora! (*To JUSTIN*) Not a word to anyone else.—I've only heard this minute, Nora. And truly, I'm more glad than I can say!—'Though Rose would never have fallen out with me, you see, if she hadn't been bitten with your mania for truth, you know,—the dazzling truth in all manner of damned little details.—

But I take it all back. (*Joyously*) And I beg your pardon. You know I'm awfully fond of you, Nora. Always was.— When she knows you're going to marry Justin——

HONORA.   Ah!

JUSTIN.   Had to tell him, Dear.——

RUFUS.   Really had to!—*You* settle down; and *she'll* settle down; and we'll all live happily ever after, and never tell the truth again!—I'm mighty glad.—On my honor, I am. You were bound to marry one of us. I'm proud to have you for a sister. Better late than never! There.—(*Enfolds* HONORA *in a brotherly hug to the bitter wrath of* JUSTIN, *and kisses her left ear which is all that's visible of her face.* HONORA *takes flight, hatless*)

HONORA.   Oh, Rufus! I—good-bye!

JUSTIN.   Don't go—You've left your hat. Honora!—(*Exit* RUFUS *joyously to the house* L.) Confound him!

HONORA.   (*Waving him away, hysterically*) No, no—I can't stop. Don't come.—I'm going.

JUSTIN.   You wanted to tell me something.

HONORA.   Yes, I did. But I don't.—I must. But I can't.—To-morrow!—I must think:—I must go, I must run away.—To-morrow! To-morrow. (*Hastens out* C.)

(JUSTIN *holding her hat, bewildered.* RUFUS *re-enters* L. *to shake his hand once more in a burst of jubilation.*)

CURTAIN.

ACT III.

SCENE I:—*The following evening—The library is lighted and the curtains are drawn. Door to the House* L. *wide. A wood-fire burning on the hearth. The high-backed sofa is drawn to face the fireplace. A lighted lamp on the table* L. *Flowers about.* HONORA'S *hat on the head of Hermes as in* ACT II.

(*Enter* L. HONORA *in feverish haste. She is in evening dress; throws her fan and gloves upon the table, and pushes her hair back from her temples, with distracted relief. She sees her Hat, catches it from Hermes and goes to the right-hand cabinet and stuffs the Hat in, on top of her MSS.—Then she looks at the house-door watchfully; and at the MSS.*)

HONORA. " *You had to dig it out of some man's heart. And Justin was the man to let you do it*". (*Between her teeth*) Yes,—he was. (*Shuts cabinet quickly*)

(*Enter* L. ROSE, MRS. SHUTTLEWORTH *and* MRS. VAN WYCK *followed by* THOMAS *the man with the coffee tray, which he passes and leaves upon a low table near* ROSE. MRS. VAN WYCK *slender, silly and of uncertain age, an exaggeration of* RUFUS' *portrait in* ACT II—*utters no laughter at present. She gazes about with vacant smiles and an attempt to be interested.* ROSE *triumphant but nervous.* MRS. SHUTTLE-WORTH *politely hostile.*)

ROSE. This is my brother-in-law's work-shop, dear Mrs. Van Wyck. (*Hastily to* HONORA, *aside*) Isn't it fearful?—You look worn out.

HONORA. I am.

MRS. VAN WYCK. (*With vacant rapture*) And this is where he writes!—How quaint—ah yes! And it will be so interesting, so Intimate, to remember this room, when one reads Mr. Hopefar's new book,—the—ah—*Aspects of Youth,*—is it not? (*Cuddling up to* MRS. SHUTTLEWORTH *upon the smaller settle, down* R. MRS. SUNTTLEWORTH *turns towards her with an effort*)

MRS. SHUTTLEWORTH. Eh?

MRS. VAN WYCK. (*Loudly*) *Aspects of Youth!*

MRS. SHUTTLEWORTH. What is the point?

HONORA. Aspects of *Truth;* the merest matter of a rhyme! (*Clock peals nine*)

MRS. VAN WYCK. Ah, what a sweet clock! I'm so devoted, you know, to all old things.

MRS. SHUTTLEWORTH. (*Putting up her fan*) I didn't quite catch——?

MRS. VAN WYCK. (*In a high voice*) I was merely saying, I'm so devoted to All Old Things!

MRS. SHUTTLEWORTH. (*Glaring at* HONORA *and ignoring* MRS. VAN WYCK) Indeed?—Pray, my dear Honora,—is it really true that this book of yours has something to do with Truth-telling?

MRS. VAN WYCK. *How quaint!*

HONORA. Yes, something. But then, it's a work of fiction, you know.

MRS. SHUTTLEWORTH. Oh, this generation has such talent for making a cat's cradle of a simple matter!

MRS. VAN WYCK. But how quaint!

MRS. SHUTTLEWORTH. Eh? Quaint and useless; like a spinning-wheel in a modern drawing-room.

MRS. VAN WYCK. Ah, do you think so? Now I'm so devoted to old things.

MRS. SHUTTLEWORTH. What's that?

Mrs. Van Wyck. I simply cannot be torn from (*Shrieking*) such sweet Old Things! (*Smiles about the room*)

Mrs. Shuttleworth. (*To* Honora) Apparently, it requires personal violence. (Rose *draws* Mrs. Van Wyck *away*) Will you exert your modern intelligence, and tell me why my niece invited this person to meet *me?* Am I the object of her antiquarian interest? (Mrs. Van Wyck's *laugh revives brilliantly, in arpeggios*) That means, the Men are coming!

(*Enter* l. Rufus, Reverend Sylvester, Justin, Carrick, Thomas Ph. D., *and* Major Kilmayne *with* Walter.)

Reverend. (*Entering*) Not at all—not at all! On the contrary, I'm sure we have missed something better worth hearing.—Although, dear lady,— (*Advancing towards* Mrs. Van Wyck) this after-dinner table now-a-days is apt to degenerate into the merest—er—*Quack—quack—Baa—baa! Pour ainsi dire!*

Mrs. Van Wyck. (*Laughing*) So quaint of you!

Thomas. (l. *to* Honora) How singuarly absent-minded! Do you know, I'm quite positive I heard you say that yesterday to Mr. Sylvester. But he seems not to recall it.

Carrick. (*To* Honora) Really, you know, you'll have to read copy-right law.

Thomas. You have such a gift of humor. (A rare gift, that,—of humor) And you are always—er—scattering about little *mots* like—er—a—pearls, —as the saying goes, before—er—a——

Honora. (*Debonairly*) But what is one to do, if one utters nothing but pearls——

Kilmayne. (*Near by*)—'Aw!

HONORA. And meets chiefly—er——

THOMAS. (*With loud eagerness*) "*Swine!*" Yes, yes.—Er—(*Takes sudden thought; looks at her again, and takes his coffee-cup away with dignity, to a corner, where he thinks it over, frowningly*)

KILMAYNE. (*Laughing*)—'aw!—'Aw!—'Aw.

MRS. SHUTTLEWORTH. (*To* RUFUS R.) I observe that your Centaur has opened his mouth at last. What did he say?

RUFUS. (*Looking at* ROSE)—'Aw! (*Who draws near*)

MRS. SHUTTLEWORTH. What else?

RUFUS. —'*Aw*—'*Aw!*—You are very exacting. All men can't talk well. He's a man of action. He can ride.

MRS. SHUTTLEWORTH. "Like a Centaur!" Yes, I know.

WALTER. (R.) And so, every time he opens his mouth,——

MRS. SHUTTLEWORTH. Do not repeat that worn expression. I am not devoted to old things.——

WALTER. This isn't old. It's greatly improved. I was going to tell you that every time he opens his mouth, being a centaur, he puts four feet in it!

MRS. SHUTTLEWORTH. Ugh!

ROSE. Wat, you are not very gracious about our guests.

WALTER. Ah, now!—Let me be helpful. Which? —Mrs. Van——

ROSE. No. Let Rufus entertain Mrs. Van Wyck. Talk to Major Kilmayne. He's more your style.

WALTER. Mine!—well, *a man's a man for a' that.* (*Crosses* L. *and joins the group around* HONORA. REVEREND *is saying*)

REVEREND. And does this novel of yours, Honora, exalt your extraordinary views of matrimony?

HONORA. Perhaps. But most of all, it exalts——
CARRICK. What indeed?
HONORA. Single Blessedness.
KILMAYNE. 'Aw! (*Incredulously*)
REVEREND. Oh, the New Woman, the New Woman! The dear, dear Selfish thing!
HONORA. Surely, surely,—Single Blessedness is better far than . . . . Double Cussedness?
KILMAYNE. (*Delighted*)—'Aw!—'Aw!—'Aw!
WALTER. (*To him*) You will lose all your idealism, Kilmayne, all of it, if you listen to these cynical opinions. (*Drawing him aside towards* ROSE)
KILMAYNE. 'Aw—'Aw! "Double Cussedness!"
WALTER. Come.
KILMAYNE. Deuced clever girl.—'Aw!
WALTER. She is that.
KILMAYNE. Never'd know she wrote books.
WALTER. Why not?
KILMAYNE. So deuced clever. 'Aw!—Never read, myself. No time.
WALTER. Perfect waste of time.
KILMAYNE. Why don't she marry?
WALTER. (*After a pause*) Too deuced clever.
KILMAYNE. "Double"—'aw—'aw!
WALTER. (*Thoughtfully to himself*) "Stands on his hinder legs with listening ear."
ROSE. (*Sweetly*) Do take Major Kilmayne to talk to Mrs. Van Wyck, dear. I've bored her horribly. She won't laugh for me. (*They join* MRS. VAN WYCK *whose laugh rings higher*)
RUFUS. (*To* JUSTIN) See here.—Did I ever strike you as an imaginative Man?
JUSTIN. No.
RUFUS. Well, I was.
JUSTIN. That wasn't Imagination. It was Youth. (*He draws* ROSE *nearer*)—Aren't you both glad that you rebounded?—Ah, laugh, Sis, laugh!

Rose. You mean, that for me, Truth is always to be incongruous and comic?

Justin. You're not calling Kilmayne comic? Haven't you any reverence for a young girl's idealism?

Rufus. Oh, but she'll laugh yet, when I tell her——

Justin. Hush.——

(Rose *crosses, pettishly to* Mrs. Van Wyck *and speaks;* Reverend *joins* Mrs. Shuttleworth r. *and speaks.*)

Mrs. Shuttleworth. Oh, it comes and goes. It is very trying, certainly.

Rose. Mrs. Van Wyck is going to *sing* for us.

Mrs. Shuttleworth. But there are compensations.

Reverend. No doubt,—no doubt! How very sweetly you take it.

Rose. I've heard so much of Mrs. Van Wyck's voice.—And now—so good of you!—we are to hear it! Shall we go to the music room?—(*Leading the way, to* Rufus) Mrs. Van Wyck is going to sing.

(*Exeunt* l. Rose, Mrs. Van Wyck Kilmayne, Mrs. Shuttleworth *and* Reverend.)

Justin. (*Slapping* Rufus *on the shoulder*) Come. Face the music! (*Outside, a chord on the piano, a prelude. To* Carrick) Come you Epicurean; come and share the hardships of the world.

(*Exeunt* Justin, Rufus, Carrick. Honora *delays. Anon, a dramatic soprano uplifted in romantic song. A door within, closed suddenly, cuts it off.*)

Walter. What's up? You're so funny this evening, Nora. You look used up; and you're talking like a riddle-book.

HONORA. Yes—So I am.—But don't wait for me. I want to stay here later. I have something more to do—to the book;—truly. And I'll let—I'll let Mr. Thomas take me home.

WALTER. Thomas!—Turn his head completely. Be advised. No? Think twice, then. *I won't* tell him. I positively won't. (*Exit* L.)

(HONORA *darts towards the right-hand cupboard. Re-enter* CARRICK L. *She turns away.*)

CARRICK. I see no reason why we should exert ourselves further. Let's join the choir invisible. (*Coming down*) May I tell you?—You're very lovely, this evening.

HONORA. Oh, do.—It's so like what they say in Books. Rose insists that men don't talk that way in Real Life.

CARRICK. Ah! Either men don't talk that way to Rose——

HONORA. Or this isn't Real Life! (*Laughs and sits down*)

CARRICK. Justin—takes it for Real Life, you know.

HONORA. Justin?

CARRICK. Yes. For him, the *Chameleon* is all rainbow color to-day. He's radiant; like a Romeo. It's a marvel to me how you've managed to—er—do it. And you so—*distraite!*

HONORA. I thought I was lovely to behold this evening! Now you admit like Rose, that I look tired out.

CARRICK. All the more beautiful. You are as disquieting and double as Mona Lisa.—And Justin, our sage, doesn't know it.

HONORA. Doesn't he?

CARRICK. Not he! Only yesterday, he rather resented my reading of you. For him, you are the soul of single purpose; and your one desire is to follow the Truth, and see where it takes you. Good old Justin!—It's charming. Far be it from me to poke fun at Justin. He's an original. Besides,— I'm on his hands to-night. I can't laugh at him till to-morrow. May I run over and see you, by the bye,—early?

HONORA. Oh, as early as you will.

CARRICK. Thanks. Maybe, you know, I shan't laugh then. For I don't know the end of the story.

HONORA. *The Chameleon?*

CARRICK. Yes; the end of the Chameleon.

HONORA. No. No, I believe you don't. That's one thing you've helped me to,—a new ending.

CARRICK. Might one know if it is good or bad?

HONORA. Both.

CARRICK. Ah, you do keep us guessing. Well, I'll wait; until to-morrow. And don't forget my counsel.

HONORA. You think I'm very double, don't you?

CARRICK. O blessed Singleness! did I say that? I mean merely, you are a woman with a mind.

HONORA. Let me tell you then: I believe you have made me see Justin . . . for the first time.

CARRICK. That's candid.

HONORA. (*Doggedly*) On the contrary, it's as double as anything can be! But you have shown me much about Justin, and about myself. And I— I thank you.

CARRICK. When the New Woman tries to hit it off with the old Adam you know,—something goes to pieces.

HONORA. Yes, something.

(*Re-enter* JUSTIN L.)

JUSTIN. You're wanted, Honora.

CARRICK. And I? (*Rising*)

JUSTIN. They clamor for you in the music-room.

HONORA. Yes, yes, of course. I ought to go back. (*Rising*)

(*Exit* CARRICK L. HONORA *crosses* L. JUSTIN *bars the way, coming down.*)

JUSTIN. I want you.—Never mind the others. Oh, I thought this thing would never be over. Not a word with you since yesterday,—a thousand days ago;—since you ran away through the garden, with your words unspoken, and good heavens! . . . Rufus, Rufus—to think of *Rufus*—kissing you!

HONORA. Oh, no, no, no! He didn't. It was just the very edge of my ear, somewhere. It didn't happen.

JUSTIN. It was torment. How can you understand? And the poor fool didn't know—what a poor fool stood looking on! That, at least I won't stand again.

HONORA. But Justin— Wait,—listen! I have so wanted to speak to you—all to-day; and yesterday . . . about—about—the Book.

JUSTIN. Ah, don't waste this moment, now!—(*He takes her in his arms. She stands with her face hidden on his breast, while he goes on, exultantly*) I have waited so long. I have thought of you—and looked at you—and loved you—as all bright dreams—as youth; and Truth and Honor,—and Life. But to hold you here,—something like a woman, I suppose, . . . more like a stray child, . . . to live and die for!—My love.

(*He lifts her face from his coat, looks down an instant on her shut eyelids; and kisses her. HONORA blindly releases herself, and reaches towards the back of a chair, with a little moan.*)

HONORA. Ah—Justin!—(*In a struggling voice*) I have tried to tell you. I have tried . . . Now I must,—I *must*.

JUSTIN. Honora——?

HONORA. Oh, how *can* I tell you?

JUSTIN. You can tell me anything, my dearest;— as you always have.

HONORA. Yes, yes, I *have* told you the truth, haven't I? in all manner of small things. Always!

JUSTIN. Always.

HONORA. But they were so small.—The great thing, Justin,—all summer long—has not been true. —And I half knew it! I half knew it! Only I couldn't tell you. I let you go on believing.

JUSTIN. Believing . . . that you loved me?

HONORA. Yes, I let you think that. I was possessed to know—to know—. To know what people and things are; and what a man's heart is; and what he thinks . . . a woman may be!

JUSTIN. Ah!

HONORA. (*Passionately*) You are the only creature I ever saw, who trusted me as I longed to be trusted. And that belief alone was so beautiful to me,—so beautiful, I came to forget what it was that you believed in. And I—made use of you! I let you love me. I adorned myself with your love, because it made me *feel* all-beautiful:—as we long to be.—I myself.—I did so love to be loved!——

JUSTIN. Oh, child——

HONORA. And I did not know—what Love— was.—I pretended. Yes, yes, I pretended all the time.—I don't myself know how much!—It was all such a new world. I seemed to walk, and see, and be myself, for the first time. I looked at the world through your mind. I made the Book of you;— that wretched Book! I wrote it, like a thief,—out of your mind and heart. . . . These last few days,——

JUSTIN. I see.

HONORA. I have been so wretched. I tried to find words . . .

JUSTIN. I see.

HONORA. I might even have let it all go on. But something opened my eyes.

JUSTIN. Opened your eyes?——

HONORA. To the fraud I had been. *I*—Truth,— and bright dreams, and honor! Dreams, if you like, that have no home—and deserve no home!—But Truth,—*I!*

JUSTIN. Something opened your eyes. And you learned——

HONORA. That I had never known—before . . . what Love is.—I have taken that name in vain.

JUSTIN. Then it was all—*mirage.*

HONORA. (*Repressing herself*) It was all . . . oh, I shall atone. Believe that:—I shall atone.

JUSTIN. There is no question of atonement.

HONORA. There is: and it is mine. Oh, go away, Justin; go away. (*Wildly*) I have said enough. I do not want to say more.

JUSTIN. My child, I will not trouble you.

(HONORA *bursts into tears. He makes a step to-ward her but she motions him away.*)

HONORA. No, no.—Justin, I implore you,—go away. I do not want to say more. *I must not!*— Heaven knows I want to—I want to. But I will not!

(JUSTIN *turns back from the garden-door.*)

JUSTIN. There must be something here I do not understand. If it is your will to leave me blind, I will go. But one word.—Is this the truth, *now?* Or am I dreaming?

HONORA. It is true. Go away—go away!

JUSTIN. Is it all? Are you telling me the *whole truth*, now?

HONORA. No!—Not even now! *Not the whole truth:—no—no—no!* (*He turns and goes out by the garden door.* HONORA *hears the door close; springs up, drying her eyes feverishly, and tries to calm herself. Then she crosses* R. *to the cup-board that holds her MSS. and pauses, with her hand on the lock*)

(*Re-enter* L. *from the house,* THOMAS Ph. D., *with his hat and coat in his hands.*)

THOMAS. You look as if you were thinking of something so interesting, I hope you'll forgive me for interrupting. Won't you?

HONORA. (*Faintly*) Oh—oh, of course. I— How do you do? I thought everyone had gone— home.

THOMAS. (*Delightedly*) Yes, everyone else has! I'm always perfectly sure, you know, to stay and lock up the house! You see, I heard you say that you thought of staying here in the library, late; and I thought it would be perhaps my last opportunity. (*Taking his thesis out of his overcoat pocket*) . . . If it won't bore you!

HONORA. Oh, how could it! (*Despairing*)

THOMAS. You're so very gracious.—Really, I shall be indebted to you.—So I said good-night to our hostess; and indeed I believe she thinks I *have* gone home! But I couldn't resist making one more effort—to get your opinion on my thesis. I have it here—in my overcoat pocket; that is, a portion of it. (*Archly*) You won't run away from me, now, —will you?

HONORA. (*Meekly*) Oh, no, indeed.—I—I'm too—too tired to run.

THOMAS. You know, your humor always seems to me the most delightful thing. Somehow, you have· the gift of drawing me out, as no one else does. I'm a bit diffident,—socially, as a rule. But with you, never!——

HONORA. (*Keeping well to the right and trying to conceal her tears*) Oh, really?—How warm it is. Shall we—turn down the lights? My eyes are —a bit—tired. (*She turns out the lamp* R. *and points to the chair and table* L. C. *for* THOMAS) Don't you want to sit there, by the lamp?—·And er —read me a—a page or two? And I will stay here, where the light doesn't hurt—my eyes. (*Stifling a sob. She sits upon the sofa before the fire so that the high back conceals her. She curls up there against the cushions, facing front*)

THOMAS. But I can't see you!

HONORA. But I can hear, perfectly.—And I—·it feels—a little—cold.

THOMAS. Indeed, indeed! (*He sits* L. C. *beside the lamp, bustling over his papers; and at length begins on the title, with elaborate emphasis. Just before, someone outside begins to play softly, on the piano. The music comes dimly*)

(HONORA, *exhausted, tucks up her feet on the sofa also, and sinks back, the picture of desolation. Her eyes shut*) The—ah—subject, of course, I have told you.—" The Influence of Imperfect Co-ordination of the Cerebral Hemispheres on some Phenomena resembling Conscious Unveracity, oc-curring in the Lower Vertebrates: Based upon a Sympathetic Study of the Psychic Processes of the Guinea-Pig." (*Music goes on softly*) Hm—yes, yes. I think that may be called thoroughly inclu-sive. " Influence—Co-ordination—Cerebral Hemi-spheres, of course—Phenomena *resembling* Con-scious Unveracity—Lower Vertebrates. Based upon a *Smpathetic* study of the Psychic Processes of the Guinea-Pig." (*Music stops*) Ah, now we can be undisturbed!—I must say that I have no fondness for reading science to a musical accompaniment. It may be all very well for *Enoch Arden*. But it must needs be most disconcerting to you and me. I fear this paragraph has been lost upon you.— Shall I—er—re-read it?—(*Silence from* HONORA) No trouble at all, I assure you. I should enjoy it. But first, do tell me if the title seems to *you* quite comprehensive. (*Silence*) Off-hand, you know. Of course it takes time and thought. Oh, don't give it too much thought you know. Awfully good of you!—May I take that as a compliment? Thank you so much.—Oh, don't weigh it too heavily, you know! I should like very much, as a specialist, to know precisely how that title will strike the lay mind. You are doubtful?—Tell me, I beg. Shall I re-read it?—Perhaps you'd like to cast your eye upon it yourself. Quite so; quite so!—(*Rises and cross* R. *with his MSS. Her silence strikes him. He adjusts his glasses, uneasily and walks around the settle, looks at her with bitter incredulity. She is asleep. Pause.*)

(*Overcome with vexation,* THOMAS Ph. D. *tiptoes away, glares at the house-door* L. *and the garden-door* C.—*listens, looks, bundles up his thesis, jealously. Then with one parting look, he puts on his overcoat, takes his hat, and with an air of offended dignity, goes out* C., *by the garden door.*)

(*Enter* L. *from the house,* THOMAS *the butler with a lighted candle, to lock up. He bars the windows and door* C., *draws the curtains, looks about, without seeing* HONORA; *puts out the lamps; and taking with him a forgotten coffee-cup from the table, goes out* L., *to the house, locking the door behind him, audibly.*)

(*The stage is dark; save for a gleam of fire-light,* HONORA *sleeps. The voice of the cuckoo peals twelve o'clock.*)

CURTAIN.

(*The curtain remains down for one moment only.*)

SCENE II:—*The same. Stage dark, save for a gleam of fire-light.* HONORA *asleep. The cuckoo-clock sounds twice.* HONORA *stirs, turns, wakes, and sits up, dazed. She looks at the fire and round the room, uttering faint exclamations of dismay as she realizes the situation.*

HONORA. Oh—? (*She springs up and feels her way to the door* C. *shut and bolted; then to the house-door* L. *locked on the other side*) Oh! (*Wildly under-breath crossing to the table near the fireplace* R.) Where was that candle? Where *was* that candle?

(*Finding the candle, she takes it, and lights it with frantic haste, from the wood-fire. Then she steals over to the house-steps and inspects the clock with another horror-stricken*) Oh!—

(*She comes down, evidently trying to piece things together and account for the situation; looks at the table where* THOMAS *had sat, and shakes her fist at them darkly*) That was how!—that was how!—But why didn't they find me?—Oh, I see, I see. And I never asked him. And they thought I'd gone home. And nobody found me.—And I'm glad. I'm not worth looking for! (*Sobbing*) And here I am, here I am again,—like a b–bad Penny. (*Desolately*)—Oh!—(*Cuckoo-clock sounds once, for* 2:30 *a. m.*) Oh, you silly bird,—I'm sorry! I didn't mean it. I'm glad you're not deaf and dumb after all. Oh good-bye, you idiotic creature!

(*Stands up resolutely, with a sudden thought*)

Good. I have been trying to do it, all these days. Now I'm locked in, with my penance! I will do it now. I will do it now. (*She puts her arms around the bust of Hermes and weeps upon his shoulder*) Oh—Oh—good-bye, you stupid lovely thing. I'll never tease you with my hateful hat any more.

(*Crossing* R. *she pauses before the left-hand cupboard that holds* JUSTIN'S *MSS. and kisses her hands which she presses against the door*) Ah— Justin's Beautiful Book!—I don't dare kiss you— But do forgive me. You shall see—

(*She backs away; draws a long breath, then goes quickly to her own cup-board; takes out first her Hat, which she shakes off, on the floor—then the MSS. of her Book. She gathers it into her hands, with alternate scorn and longing*) Ah—you miserable Sinner,—you poor, poor—darling—oh—(*Kissing it madly*) How can I? How can I?—Yes, I can. I can. (*Fiercely*) And I will—I will—I will. It's the only way. It's all I have.—

(*She holds it close against her breast for a moment, with her face set. Then mutters*) Good-bye—good-bye—good-bye—!

(*She throws it into the fireplace; then kneels down, and with her arm before her eyes, heaps paper and ashes together; and revives the flame with the bellows. It flares up. Sound of a hand on the house-door knob. Then the key grates in the lock.* HONORA *starts up like a deer; blows out her candle instantly; and crouches between the high settle and the fireplace, peering with great eyes*)

(*The house-door* L. *opens. Enter* JUSTIN. *He is still in evening dress and carries a lighted candle. He shuts the door behind him and comes down, slowly, his face pale and set. Mechanically, he places his candle on the table* L. C. *and crosses* R. *and sits, facing* HONORA'S *old place down* L.)

(HONORA R. *meanwhile creeps on her hands and knees behind the settle, up towards the back of the stage, and watches frm her hiding-place with more and more wonder and misery.* JUSTIN *disturbed by evident reminiscence, turns away slightly, and looks into space, evidently taking some resolve. Then with a sharp sigh, he rises suddenly, and turns to his left-hand cabinet.* HONORA *creeps* c. *as he turns* R.)

(*He opens the cupboard and takes out his MS.; holds it a moment, thinking—then he goes towards the fireplace. He sits upon the settle facing it.*)

(HONORA *watches with horrified amazement.*)

(*He takes a handful of pages and puts them in the fire*)

(HONORA *springs out of hiding and falls on her knees by the edge of the settle, catching his arm.* HONORA, *piteously*) No, no!—no, no—no, no!

(JUSTIN, *violently startled, turns and sees her, then he rises.*)

JUSTIN. You—Honora!—Here? What does this mean?

HONORA. I don't know.

JUSTIN. Why are you not at home?

HONORA. I don't know. I meant to go home; but nobody took me. I mean—I went to sleep, somehow. And nobody found me. (*He stands looking at her in deep perplexity. She replies, equally dazed, like a tired child*) When I woke up, I was here, locked in.

JUSTIN. You poor child.

HONORA. (*Weeping*) Oh, don't—don't say that, after all I have been. I cannot bear it!

JUSTIN. I must take you home.

HONORA. Oh, don't—don't take me home! No one has missed me, yet. I'll go, whenever it's light.

But your Book,—your Book. What were you going
to do to your Book?

JUSTIN.   (*Laying aside the MS. on the settle*)
Oh, never mind the book.   Of course I did not
dream that you were here.

HONORA.   Tell me the truth.   You were going to
burn it?

JUSTIN.   (*After a pause*)   Yes.   I'm going to
burn it.

HONORA.   (*Stifling a scream*)   Justin, no, no!—
Oh, Justin, it is not like you, to be so cruel.

JUSTIN.   Cruel?

HONORA.   You mean, it is ruined; because there
was so much of me there, as you said.

JUSTIN.   Oh, my child, do you think I burn it, to
be cruel?

HONORA.   No,—no.   But why do you want to
burn it?   Why,—why?   Tell me.   I can stand it.
I must know.

JUSTIN.   Why,—I meant to burn it, because it
seemed to me . . . worthless.

HONORA.   Not true?   Not true?

JUSTIN.   Not true.

HONORA.   Because of me!

JUSTIN.   Don't.   Let us say: It is not the book
I meant to write.   It is not the book I thought I had
written.   Surely you understand that.   Let us call
the whole thing a dream, merely.   But let me burn
up, now—everything that was not—Real.   (*Takes
the MS. up.   With a cry, HONORA flings herself
upon it, and takes it from him*)   Honora!

HONORA.   Come away.   Come away from the fire.
I'll tell you all.   But you must promise me not to
burn it.   You will *kill* me, if you burn it.   You will
put me out of the world!   I'll tell you all.

JUSTIN.   All——?

HONORA.   You know I told you, last night, it was
not the whole truth; not the whole.   But you shall

have the whole truth now. Because it's my penance, and I must. Now that you care no longer,—
now that I've ruined the book;—now that I'm
none of those things you loved me for,—now that
I'm dethroned——

JUSTIN. Honora!

HONORA. (*Tonelessly*) It's now,—I love you.
I love you. I never knew what it meant—before.
(JUSTIN *takes a step towards her, never moving his
eyes from her face. She shrinks from him a little;
then goes on*) I tried so not to tell you, last night.
For I knew you would try then, to make it all seem
well,—for my sake. And I had not been Real—
until then. It's not easy. (*She catches his intense,
sad look and cries*) Oh—you don't believe me!

JUSTIN. I try to understand. But—child——

HONORA. I tell you, now,—only to save the Book.

JUSTIN. Yes.—That's only too clear.

HONORA. Clear?—You—don't believe me? Oh,
I see, (*brokenly*) I see. How childish of me. But
I'll make you understand. Didn't I know you well
enough, to know that you could never love me,
when you learned of my pretending all this summer
long? Oh, yes, I knew that well. But these last
few days, my eyes were opened to what I had been
doing. I saw myself. And I saw you. And then,
last night, . . . I loved you. And I saw that I had
never understood, before.

JUSTIN. Honora——

HONORA. So don't punish this! (*Holding out
the Book*) I tell you only for penance. And—I've
burned—mine.

JUSTIN. What do you mean? You've burned
what?

HONORA. My Book. He said I had written it
out of your heart. And that was true.—I didn't
know what love was, though I'd said so much about
it. Now I know. It's—This. (*She adds vacantly*)

So I—burned the Book. (JUSTIN *turns to the fire-place and catches up, with incredulous pain, a hand-ful of scraps. As he turns back to her, speechless,* HONORA, *half smiling*) You see, there's nothing left but the Truth; and this. (*Touching his Book wistfully. He catches it from her*)

JUSTIN.   Nothing—nothing—nothing but the truth! (*He tosses the book into the fireplace, catches* HONORA *in his arms and holds her there, fast*)

HONORA. (*Struggling*) The Book—Justin!

JUSTIN. I have the truth. I have you. I want nothing more—nothing—nothing!

HONORA. It was so Beautiful!

JUSTIN. Not beautiful enough.

HONORA. Oh, it was true!

JUSTIN. Not true enough.

HONORA. Oh, what will you have?

JUSTIN. Say it—say it.

HONORA. I love you—I love you. You are everything I have in the world.

JUSTIN. Ah! (*They fold each other in. After a pause,* JUSTIN *says radiantly*) Was anything ever true before?

HONORA. No. I feel new-born. Ah, but your Book!

JUSTIN. Who wants it? I'll begin a better one to-morrow. We'll both begin—To-day! (*Looking at the clock*) Do you know, it's morning! The First Morning!

HONORA. And you are the first Man I ever saw.

JUSTIN. Ah, I knew you long ago, for the First Woman. And you've come true!

(*Cuckoo-clock peals four.*)

HONORA. Oh, that disgracefully early bird!

JUSTIN.   Oh, darling—Worm! (*Embracing*

her) What shall I do for you? You Child—tired, hungry, cold, lost.

HONORA. Must I go home?

JUSTIN. Home? I am home; and I am he. (*Unhooks a portière from the French window up* R.) Here is a cloak for you. (*Wraps it around her. Blows out his candle. Pushes back the curtains. It is dawn outside*) Now then;—Food! Shall I rouse them?

HONORA. No, no!

JUSTIN. Look out. (*They go to the window together*) Behold—the garden of Eden!—And yon herd of beautiful beasts,—golden and cinnebar— stars on their foreheads:—horns of pearl! What do you call that creature, Eve? It isn't a river-horse, surely.

HONORA. Let it be named Cow, my dearest.

JUSTIN. And shall I—I have it! (*Suddenly*) Something to eat!—Grapes, grapes, growing all over the summer-house!

(*Exit* R. C. *through the French window—Stage grows lighter.* HONORA *calls softly.*)

HONORA. Don't be gone—long. I'm afraid, all alone . . in such a new world; and the very first morning!

(*She turns back to the room with a rapturous sigh: goes up to Hermes and hugs him*)

(*Re-enter* JUSTIN *with grapes and leaves.*)

JUSTIN. Come from the thing of clay! (*She turns to him and sees her Hat on the floor*)

HONORA. I'll burn that, too. The deceitful thing, all frills and pretences!

JUSTIN.   No, no!—Books if you will. But not
the Hat!

HONORA. Yes, I will burn my Hat, too! (*Stuffs
it in the fire.*) I will!

JUSTIN. Eat,—eat! I have brought you the best
of Eden.   (*Voices in the house* L.)—By Jove,
they're up.

HONORA. Oh, oh, the time, the explanations!

(JUSTIN *rushes to the cuckoo-clock.*)

JUSTIN. Shall it be early or late? Speak. It's
any time you like.—It's the golden age. (*He twists
the hands backward, forward, round, recklessly to
six.   The cuckoo shrills and keeps on shrilling;
voices approach*)

HONORA. Oh, Justin—the bird, the bird! You've
upset him altogether!

(JUSTIN *hastens down the steps, and stands before
HONORA, down* R. C., *who is still enveloped in
her curtain and shaking with laughter. The
Cuckoo chirrups without intermission during
the rapid dialogue and chorus that follows:
The house-door* L. *opens, admitting* RUFUS, *in
the evening dress of* ACT III. ROSE, *likewise,
with a long wrap;* WALTER, *dishabille and ul-
ster;* CARRICK *in a great coat; last of all,*
THOMAS Ph. D., *in miscellaneous lendings.
They stand huddled on the steps* L. *and all
speak together.*)

ROSE.	It was certainly here.
CARRICK.	Never knew it was an alarm-clock
	as well——
RUFUS.	Saw him getting in the window!
WALTER.	By Jove. Nobody here!

(*A pause. Then.*)

ROSE.	Honora!——
RUFUS.	Justin!——
WALTER.	Honora!——
CARRICK.	Most unexpected!——

WALTER. In the name of wonder, Honora! You look as if you'd been out all night!
HONORA. I—I have!

(THOMAS Ph. D., *appears* L. *on the upper step, clad in a bath-robe and spectacles and with an umbrella in his hand.*)

THOMAS. Oh, dear me, how perfectly extraordinary! I hope I don't intrude.

(*They turn.*)

RUFUS. By Jove, no. Glad to see you. Had no idea you were staying.
THOMAS. Er—no. You see I stayed later than I intended. And I missed the last train. So I came back; and Walter very kindly put me up—and lent me——
WALTER. Don't mention 'em——
THOMAS. And lent me——
WALTER. Yes, yes!

(*They all turn back to* JUSTIN *and* HONORA.)

THOMAS. But I had no idea you were in the habit of rising so early!
JUSTIN. In a word,—Honora's burned out!

(HONORA *hides her laughter in the portière. A speedy chorus follows.*)

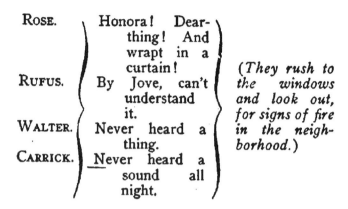

ROSE.
RUFUS.
WALTER.
CARRICK.

Honora! Dear-thing! And wrapt in a curtain! By Jove, can't understand it. Never heard a thing. Never heard a sound all night.

(*They rush to the windows and look out, for signs of fire in the neighborhood.*)

JUSTIN. —I'll tell you the whole thing. But not a word until she's fed and rested. Go, get up Thomas; Honora's cold and hungry.

CHORUS. —Of course!—Quite right.—Never heard a thing!—Don't see how it happened.

THOMAS. (*Lifting his nose, like a pointer*) Yes, yes,—I smell smoke! I smell smoke distinctly.

ROSE. (*Hurrying to* HONORA) Oh, how self-absorbed we were. I can't believe it!

HONORA. Who?

ROSE. (*To* HONORA *in a joyful whisper*) I'm so happy! (*Rufus told me!* (*Aloud*) We sat up in the arbor. Rufus and I. We—were talking it all over. And we quite forgot the hour.

RUFUS. (*Gladly*) Like a perfect Romeo and Juliet; 'Pon my word—*Saw the sun rise!*——I say, did any of you ever see the sun rise?

ROSE. And only just now, we thought we heard somebody and we looked out just in time to see——

RUFUS. *See the Sun rise!* (*Proudly*)

ROSE. —A man going through that window.

RUFUS. | So we hurried back——
WALTER. | So you roused us all up——
CARRICK. } Most adventurous morning!
THOMAS. | Oh, dear me, how very extra-
ordinary!

ROSE. (*To* HONORA) *And Justin saved you!*
And the others——
HONORA. All safe!—Yes, Justin saved me!
CARRICK. Idyllic ending, I'm sure.
HONORA. Isn't it?—*Isn't it a good ending?*
JUSTIN. (*With authority*) Come. Make a fire.
Get something to eat. Bestir, bestir! We're com-
ing.
CHORUS. That's so. Where's Thomas? Coffee!
Eggs! Quick. Tell us all about it.

(*They all scatter out, confusedly.*)

JUSTIN. (*Laughing, and pointing to the fireplace*) Honora's burned out!—But it wasn't a
Chameleon! 'Twas a phoenix. And she rises from
her own ashes—to-day! Off with your dark dis-
guise, my chrysalid! (*He lifts the portière from
her shoulders, and wreathes the grape-leaves in her
hair.*) Come, Truth,—come, Beggar-maid, and
say—
HONORA. *Ah,..good,—good Morning!*

CURTAIN.

CPSIA information can be obtained
at www.ICGtesting.com
Printed in the USA
LVHW090534010619
619855LV00012B/167/P